EASTER MAUS

There was once a small mouse in a small town called Salem, at the Edge of the Wilderness. The mouse was named Maus Kraus. She was a very smart maus: she knew how to sew, and she went to school every day with her great friend Catherine, who was the teacher in the Girls School. Sister Catherine called her Sister Maus, and you may already know about her from reading her first book. In her second book, Sister Maus learned about Christmas and discovered new ways, indeed, to be useful.

In this, her third book, Sister Maus meets Brother Peter the Potter. He lives in Bethabara, another small town at the Edge of the Wilderness. As you shall see, it is very close to Salem. Brother Peter's wife is Sister Christina, and their children are Nan and Baby Israel. They are all friends of Sister Catherine – and, of course – of Sister Maus!

Dedicated to the descendants of Peter Oliver.

EASTER MAUS

Published by Salem Academy and College
601 South Church Street, Winston-Salem, North Carolina 27101
www.salemacademy.com *and* www.salem.edu

Typeset and designed in the United States of America by Carrie Leigh Dickey
Printed and bound in the United States of America by Keiger Printing Company, Inc.
FIRST LIMITED EDITION, first printing

ISBN 978-0-9789608-2-7

EASTER MAUS

A Third Small Tale of Sisters House in Salem

by John Hutton

SALEM ACADEMY AND COLLEGE
2010

Once again it is a quiet morning long ago in Old America – and we are in Bethabara where Brother Peter the Potter lives. Brother Peter loads his wagon with straw and pots. He must take them to Sisters House in nearby Salem. "Giddup!" The horse knows the way – they will be in Salem soon.

Meanwhile, everyone in Sisters House is doing their morning chores. All of a sudden there is a tremendous noise.

KNOCK, KNOCK, KNOCK!

The Sisters House Mice are very surprised to see that it is a man, and a brother – and at the door of Sisters House! Who is it? Sister Maus would know, but where can she be?

Why, it is Brother Peter. He is a great friend of Sister Catherine, the teacher at the Little Girls School.

*Most of the pictures in this book have eggs in them, large and small, plain and decorated. See how many you can find.

"New pots, Sister Catherine! New pots for the Easter flowers!" "Thank you, Brother Peter! Thank goodness you are here. Brother Rudolph has been sick for two weeks, or we wouldn't have had to call you down from Bethabara!" "No trouble at all. I am always very glad to help."

Brother Peter puts an armload of pots on the counter. They are beautiful and red, with green and cream stripes and flowers. Sister Catherine admires them very much.

"How can we pay you, Brother Peter? Can we give you pretty embroidered gloves for Sister Christina, and little Sister Nan? Can we give you pretty ribbons and a cap for a little girl almost ready for school?" "Gloves, and pretty gloves, and ribbons and caps – for my pots? That's just what I think Nan will like best!"

Sister Catherine smiles and wraps the gloves and ribbons and caps in brown paper.

"Brother Peter! Will we see you when you come back again, this Sunday, on Easter Day?" "Yes, we shall see you – Christina, Nan, Baby and I – at sunrise, and with flowers in our hands! I am in the Easter Band, you know!"

"Then come, please come after the Sunrise Service, for breakfast with us in Sisters House!" "Yes, of course! Auf Wiedersehen! Goodbye!"

Brother Peter puts his package of gloves and ribbons and caps in his wagon. He drives across the Square to the Boys School. The boys have cracked some of their favorite mugs, and Brother Peter will take them home to fix. He stacks the mugs in soft straw, next to the gloves.

Brother Peter drives home. He worked for many years for Brother Rudolph, the Salem potter. Now he has his own pottery and farm in Bethabara, just a few miles north of Salem.

The wagon bumps over the rough roads. The brown paper jostles and rustles. Someone small wakes up. It is Sister Maus! She was up late last night embroidering and fell asleep inside one of the gloves after she stitched the last tiny stitch.

"Oh deary, deary me!" she squeaks, as she crawls out and peers over the back of the wagon at the passing trees, all flowery-white. She shakes a petal from her shoulder. "What shall I do! Sister Catherine will be missing me again, indeed she will!"

The wagon rolls up to a small farm yard. There is a barn on one side, a small and tidy house on the other, and in the middle a pottery workshop. Brother Peter pulls the wagon into the barn and goes into the house. Sister Christina, his wife, greets him in the kitchen. "Peter! Your supper is ready!"

"Daddy!" Daughter Nan gives him a big hug. Baby Israel is asleep in his crib.

Brother Peter shows them what Sister Catherine has given him. Nan is so happy.

Gloves, and pretty gloves, and ribbons, and caps – for Daddy's pots – that's just what Nan likes best!

When it is quiet in the barn, Sister Maus slides down the wagon pole and looks around. How surprised she is to see some Country Mice looking at her! They stop her when she begins to speak. "Hush-hush-hush-hush-hush-hush-hush!!!!" whisper the mice, all at once. "Be very quiet! Schnitzle and Strudel are friendly – but you must not surprise them – they might bite!"

"Grrrrrr-orrr-rrr-arrr!" Do not worry! Brother Schnitzle and Sister Strudel are very fond of mice and are very happy to have a visitor.

In the barn they also meet Anna Maria and her chicks. Cluck, cluck, cluck! She gives them a basket of eggs that did not hatch. Perhaps Nan could color them for Easter.

"Please come with us," Father Mouse says kindly, "our home is your home." Just as they turn to go, they hear a noise from the wagon. "Wait for me!" It is Brother Maus. He had fallen asleep in one of the cracked mugs Brother Peter brought from the Boys School and is now wide awake. "May I come too?" Of course! The Country Mice show Brother and Sister Maus the barn from top to bottom. It is warm and cozy and filled with hay.

The next day they visit Brother Peter's own pottery workshop. Around and around and around and again! Brother Peter is an excellent potter. His strong hands spin the clay taller and taller. Look! He has made a beautiful bowl! Brother Maus tries to make a pot, too. Oops! Very squashy!

The Country Mice help Brother Peter keep everything very clean and tidy. They are also fine painters and know many interesting designs. While they are working, Nan comes in with her embroidery.

"I can't do it!" she cries. "It is very hard!" But Sister Maus knows what to do.

Her tiny hands make tiny stitches while Nan watches. Don't give up, Nan! You can do it, too.

After the sewing lesson, they all go to Sister Christina's kitchen to color Anna Maria's eggs. Nan loves to paint Easter eggs. She shows Sister Maus how to do it. Baby Israel is still too young, but he will try.

Every night when his work is finished, Brother Peter comes to the barn to practice his trombone for the Easter service. Sister Christina does not allow practicing in the house. The Country Mice keep Brother Peter company. They are also very good musicians. Brother and Sister Maus begin to learn to play the trumpet. Blow harder, Sister Maus! Nan thinks that they all play very well.

Finally, it is Easter morning and time to go back to Salem. Sister Christina wakes every one up. It is still very early and very dark. Brother Peter loads the wagon. The mice find comfortable places snug in the hay. Nan tucks herself in and joins her little friends.

Everything is ready. They begin the trip by torchlight. Every mile they stop to play their instruments – and the mouse band plays, too! More sleepers wake up and follow the wagon to Salem.

Salem at last! It is almost dawn. Everyone is very excited and brings pots full of beautiful flowers with them. Bands walk and ride into town from every direction. They all begin to play. The sun is rising! Everyone sings. The Lord is Risen!

It is time for Easter breakfast. Sister Maus sees Sister Catherine in the crowd. She and Brother Maus crawl sleepily into her apron pocket. Brother Peter leads his horse down the street to Sisters House. "What a big town!" say the Country Mice.

The kitchen table is full of hot, delicious food – and soon, too, are all the guests. Brother Peter is pleased to see his pots and bowls put to such a good use. Little Nan gives a basket full of beautiful Easter Eggs to Sister Catherine.

Sister Catherine smiles. "We hope that Nan will come to the Little Girls School, soon!" Will she? Yes, she will!

Sister Maus introduces the new pupil to the other girls. What nice new friends! Sister Catherine gives Nan a book. It is a lovely Easter present. She will read it with her mother and be ready to come back to school next week. Now books – and more books – and gloves, ribbons and caps, and going to school – are just what Nan likes best!

Sister Maus tells the Sisters House Mice about where she has been. They are very impressed that she has learned to play the trumpet. Sister Maus always has such interesting adventures, indeed! The end.

SPECIAL THANKS

Salem Academy and College gratefully acknowledges the generous support of the Sam N. Carter and Pauline Carter Fund of the Winston-Salem Foundation and grantmaking partner Charlie Hemrick for making this book possible.

Special thanks are also due to Penny Niven, Gwynne Taylor, Jane Carmichael, Johanna Brown, Ellen Kutcher and Dr. John Raymond Oliver Jr.

AUTHOR'S NOTES

Easter Maus, like *Sister Maus* and *Christmas Maus*, is a book based on the early days of Salem Academy and College, an academic institution for women founded in 1772 in the village of Salem in the Moravian settlement of Wachovia, located in northwestern North Carolina. The Single Sisters House, where all three stories take place, still exists on the campus of Salem College in Winston-Salem, and visitors are encouraged to come to see Sister Maus's historic mouse hole! Please see the Author's Notes in *Sister Maus* and *Christmas Maus* for more historical information about Salem.

As in previous volumes, many historical threads come together to form the story of *Easter Maus*. In this book, the threads are represented by historic buildings in Salem and the nearby community of Bethabara; traditional Salem pottery and Easter eggs; symbolic flowers; the historic Moravian Easter Sunrise Service in Salem; and a fascinating eighteenth-century African-American Moravian craftsman.

The main characters in *Easter Maus* are named in honor of real people whom I admire from Salem's past. The fictional Brother Peter is loosely based on Peter Oliver, an African-American farmer and potter who lived in Salem and Bethabara. He overcame great obstacles in his life. Born a slave in Virginia in 1766, he was brought to Salem in 1785, the same year Sisters House was built. He went to Bethabara in 1788 to work for Rudolph Christ, one of Salem's finest potters, at a time when Christ had taken over the Bethabara pottery. Later, Peter Oliver worked for Gottlob Krause, Bethabara's second master potter. Oliver returned to Salem in 1796 to work with Christ again, and purchased his freedom about 1801. He married and leased a farm, and some evidence suggests he also remained a potter. He died in 1810 and is buried in God's Acre at Salem. Peter Oliver's descendants live in Winston-Salem to this day. More information on Peter Oliver can be found in: *African-Americans in Salem* by John Sensabach, a pamphlet published by Old Salem, Inc.

Little Nan in the story is named for two historical figures. One was Peter Oliver's daughter Nancy. The other was Anna Samuels, the first African-American student at Salem Female Academy, enrolled there from 1798-1801. It seemed to me that Nan could be a fine nickname for both Nancy and Anna! Sister Christina and Baby Israel are named for Peter Oliver's wife, Christina Bass, and their son, Israel.

Brother Peter's pottery workshop was inspired by rooms in the Single Brothers House in Salem, and the pottery workshop preserved in Bethabara Park, Winston-Salem. Sister Christina's kitchen in the book is modeled on the one in the Bethabara pottery. Brother Peter's barn is loosely based on the one located next to the Salem Tavern in Salem.

Historic Bethabara Park, supported by the City of Winston-Salem, preserves the site where the Moravians first settled in 1753 in Forsyth County. After many of the inhabitants of Bethabara moved to the larger town of Salem in 1772, Bethabara gradually dwindled into a smaller farming community. It is still a beautiful place to visit today, and many special events take place in the park.

Eighteenth-century Moravians were expert gardeners and loved flowers, both for their own sake and for the strong symbolic reminder they provided of Christ's sacrifice and resurrection. Roses, lilies, tulips, anemones, and lilies of the valley were special favorites, and often appear in Moravian pottery decoration. At Easter time, flowers are traditionally placed on graves in Salem's Cemetery, God's Acre, and in the story I imagined that the practice had its roots in the earliest years of the settlement. Household pottery could well have been pressed into service as temporary vases at that time.

Objects from the Old Salem Collection inspired the pottery which appears throughout the book. The molded earthenware bottles, decorated plates and various vessels seen in Brother Peter's shop and on the Easter table are examples. In some cases I took the liberty of letting Brother Peter and his small assistants paint elaborate slip decoration (designs in diluted colored clays) on vessels – pitchers, jars and jugs that would ordinarily be plainly glazed. Fancy slip-painted designs were typically reserved by Salem potters for large decorative plates.

Although no signed pots by Peter Oliver have been identified, the author's hypothesis is that this skilled potter, only a few generations removed from Africa, might have sometimes combined a West African love of pattern with European Moravian decorative traditions. More specifically, Oliver's pots might have at least occasionally resembled a small group of slip-decorated pots with geometric designs formerly attributed to Rudolph Christ and currently credited to a group of eighteenth- and nineteenth-century German Reformed potters originally from Berks County, Pennsylvania who were active not far from Salem, in Alamance County, North Carolina.

The Sunrise Service described in the book was an essential part of the eighteenth-century Moravian celebration of Easter at Salem, and the tradition continues today. The first Moravian sunrise service took place in Herrnhut, Saxony (Germany), in 1753, and the practice was brought to America by the first Moravian settlers. As in the book, brass bands begin to play very early in the morning, calling worshippers to follow and travel towards God's Acre to meet at sunrise. Eighteenth-century bands traveled to Salem by torchlight, on foot and in wagons; twenty-first-century ones reach the same destination by automobile and minivan!

The origins of coloring Easter eggs in the United States are often traced to German immigrants, including the Moravians, in the eighteenth and nineteenth centuries. Early Moravian Easter eggs were typically emptied and the hollow shells decorated, either by painting in watercolor or by using natural dyestuffs. Elaborate designs and patterns could be created through wax resist techniques as well. The decorated eggs on the endpapers were inspired by eighteenth-century pottery designs, as well as traditional motifs currently practiced in Moravia in the Czech Republic– the area from which the Salem settlers originally came. Some African-inspired designs honoring Peter Oliver's heritage are also included.

Finally, to return to Sisters House: the story begins in the Vorsteherin's (manager's) Office, a room which is immediately on the left as you enter the building through the central door facing the village Square. I imagined that this room was the perfect place for Sister Catherine to do business with Brother Peter. The inhabitants of Sisters House conducted many enterprises, including the making of the fine gloves and caps. The Easter breakfast at the end of the story takes place in the Sisters House kitchen, now part of the museum in the building. The kitchen has been left unrestored, with the floor removed, in order to show visitors something of the original construction techniques.

John Hutton was educated at Princeton, the University of London and Harvard. He has written and illustrated several books for children, including *Sister Maus* (2006) and *Christmas Maus* (2008) He has taught in the Art Department at Salem since 1990.